Kathy Lette first [...] with the novel *Puberty Blues*, which [...] a major film and a TV mini-series. After several years as a newspaper columnist and television sitcom writer in Los Angeles and New York, she wrote eleven international bestsellers including *Mad Cows* (the film starred Joanna Lumley and Anna Friel), *How to Kill Your Husband (and Other Handy Household Hints)* (recently staged by the Victorian Opera), *To Love, Honour and Betray* and *The Boy Who Fell To Earth*. Her novels have been published in fourteen languages.

Kathy appears regularly as a guest on the BBC and CNN News. She is an ambassador for Women and Children First, Plan International and the White Ribbon Alliance. In 2004 she was the London Savoy Hotel's Writer in Residence where a cocktail named after her can still be ordered. Kathy is an autodidact (a word she taught herself) but in 2010 received an honorary doctorate from Southampton Solent University.

Kathy lives in London with her husband and two children. Visit her website at www.kathylette.com and on Twitter @KathyLette.

Also by Kathy Lette

Love Is Blind

but marriage is a real eye opener

Kathy Lette

BLACK SWAN

TRANSWORLD PUBLISHERS
61–63 Uxbridge Road, London W5 5SA
A Random House Group Company
www.transworldbooks.co.uk

LOVE IS BLIND
A BLACK SWAN BOOK: 9780552779197

First publication in Great Britain
Black Swan edition published 2013

Addresses for Random House Group Ltd companies outside the UK
can be found at: www.randomhouse.co.uk
The Random House Group Reg. No. 954009

The Random House Group Limited supports The Forest Stewardship
Council® (FSC®), the leading international forest-certification
organization. Our books carrying the FSC label are printed on
FSC®-certified paper. FSC is the only forest-certification scheme
endorsed by the leading environmental organizations, including
Greenpeace. Our paper-procurement policy can be found
at www.randomhouse.co.uk/environment

Typeset in 12/16pt Stone Serif by
Kestrel Data, Exeter, Devon.
Printed and bound by
CPI Group (UK) Ltd, Croydon, CR0 4YY.

2 4 6 8 10 9 7 5 3 1

For my dear mother, Val, who introduced
me to the joy of reading

Acknowledgements

Thanks to my sister Jenny and brother-in-law Niall O'Carroll for top bush survival tips. Thanks also to my editors, Cat Cobain and Sophie Wilson for talking me off a literary ledge occasionally. And to Larry Finlay and Gail Rebuck for introducing me to the wonderful world of Quick Reads. And finally, hello to all new readers. I'm so glad you're slipping between my covers.

Chapter One

Beauty Is In The Eye Of The Beholder

'The Outback? What do you *mean* you're moving to the Australian Outback?' Anthea's startled words were lost on her sister as Jane barrelled down the stone steps to stash another suitcase into the boot of her car. '*Why*?'

'The man shortage,' Jane grunted glumly. 'All the men in London are married or gay. Or married *and* gay.' She pushed back up the stairs past her perfectly groomed elder sister to fetch more belongings from her flat.

Anthea tottered in sky-scraper high heels towards her sister's car which was parked half up on the kerb. The uneven pavement of inner-city Soho made her feel like a toddler taking to the ice. 'Weren't you even going to tell me?' she asked.

'Why bother? I knew you'd just try to talk me out of it,' Jane replied, as she strapped her cello case into the back seat. Anthea thought crossly that it was just so typical of her sister to take up the cello as a child, when a clarinet or flute would have been so much less fuss.

'Oh, well, that's just lovely, isn't it? Thank God I happened to drop by on the way home from court then . . . Otherwise I wouldn't even have known that my sister had fled the country. My legal case was settled by the way. Thanks for asking,' she added, sarcastically.

'I thought of writing to you, Anthea, but what could I say? "So glad your life's perfect . . . engaged to a legal eagle. Great job. Mortgage as small as your waist. Designer genes inherited from Mum and Dad . . . But I'm buggering off because I'm thirty-two and my eggs are rotting in my ovaries." But there just didn't seem to be a greetings card to cover that,' Jane said, sharply.

Though separated in age by only thirteen months, Anthea and Jane were not the type of sisters to sit around exchanging polite remarks. Instead they'd spent their youth using each other as dartboards. Basically the two siblings got on as well as a gun-toting hunter and an

Animal Rights supporter. Anthea felt duty-bound to express a desire that her less successful younger sister should make a go of things out in the Colonies . . . But found she secretly wanted to load Jane down with heavy weights and drop her in piranha-infested waters.

Jane, on the other hand, felt sure that if her oh, so perfect, control-freak elder sister ever ended up in a lifeboat, the other passengers would eat her by the end of the first day. Even if they had plenty of food and water and land was in sight. Just because she was so damned annoying.

Anthea stepped gingerly over the dog turds which dotted the pavement. She couldn't understand why Jane insisted on dwelling in this seedy, inner-city area. She could have bought a nice house in the outer suburbs for half the price, using the money their parents had left. It was typical of her little sister's lack of common sense.

After the tragic death of their beloved mother and father, in a boating accident in the Red Sea two years before, Anthea had tried to encourage her sister to act like an adult. But there were times when she was secretly tempted to put Jane up for adoption. 'Where exactly are you moving to on the other side of the world, if it's not too much to ask?' Anthea enquired crossly.

'Broken Ridge. Mining town. West Australia.' Jane leant on the car bonnet to catch her breath. The suitcases had been heavy. Hands on stout, denim-clad hips, she faced her slender sister. 'As you know, I've been on so many blind dates, I should be given a free guide dog. But I've been looking in the wrong places!'

Her face came alive with excitement then. 'In the Australian Outback,' she chirped, 'men outnumber women ten to one.' Jane retrieved a scrunched-up newspaper article from her pocket and thrust it at her sister.

Anthea perched her sunglasses on top of her highlighted blonde locks. She smoothed out the blurred print with her manicured claws. Then she read aloud very slowly, as though conversing with someone who was hard of hearing.

'*A mayor in the Australian Outback has called on ladies who are plain looking to move to his town. A shortage of women means the men there aren't too picky. He says, "Quite often you will see a lass here who is maybe not so attractive . . . yet she has a wide smile*

12

on her face. Perhaps she's thinking about a recent meeting with an eager man, or else is keen for the next one! If you're an ugly duckling, why not move here? Let the attention you'll receive turn you into a beautiful swan."'

Anthea glanced up at her younger sister. Jane's face shone with hope. Anthea's face, however, was rigid with anger. 'This is absolutely outrageous. It's awful! How dare this Aussie mayor judge women only by the way they look! What about character? And brains? Who cares about looks? You're so clever and funny, Jane.'

'So bloody what?' she replied tightly, her smile gone. 'Any bloke who ever liked my sense of humour ended up by falling in love with *you* instead.' She looked at her elder sister with slant-eyed hostility.

A passerby would not have picked them out as sisters. Whereas Anthea glided, Jane stomped. Anthea was trim, with a swimmer's body. The loose hammocks of flesh under Jane's mottled upper arms wobbled when she moved. Anthea was fine-featured like their mother had been. (Jane secretly thought her elder sister's nose a

13

little hawk-like which made her look predatory.) Jane knew that her own soft button of a nose was lost in her big-boned face, as though it had been stuck on with Blu-Tack.

The one thing they did share was a talent for making cutting remarks. Their tongues were sharp enough to shave your legs with.

'Women are as close to being valued for their characters as Lady Gaga is to joining a convent,' Jane declared bitterly.

'But you're very attractive, Jane – in your own way.'

Jane's eyes flashed before narrowing in a look of contempt. 'Oh, please don't treat me like a child. Do you think Mum knew all along I was going to be plain? She named you Anthea, which means flower, and then took one look at me in the crib and decided "plain Jane".'

Uncomfortable with the familiar turn their talk was taking, Anthea changed tack. 'I can't believe that Outback mayor says the town welcomes women who are "plain looking". That must make the ones who are in the town already feel just dreadful.'

Jane shrugged. 'I don't know. I think he's just being practical.'

'We all know about racism. Well, this man has face-ism,' Anthea said crisply, as if addressing an invisible jury. 'He's facially prejudiced.'

Jane's eyes glittered with spite. 'Oh, and you're not? You judge *your* man by *his* looks. You once said to me, "no pecs, no sex"'. And anyway, Rupert, your live-in Ken doll, *he* judges *you* by your looks. Do you think he'd be living with you if you looked like *me*?'

Anthea thought for a moment of her handsome, clever fiancé, Rupert. He was a successful lawyer with a big firm in the City of London. They'd been engaged for four years, which did seem rather a long time. But they'd both been too busy to organise the wedding. Let alone take time off to go on honeymoon . . . Well, it was mostly Rupert who was too busy.

Anthea was desperate to 'tie the knot', as her mother used to call it. As soon as her fiancé was made a partner in his law firm, he had promised that she would become Mrs Rupert Cavendish. It was a title she craved.

Anthea took a deep breath and then employed the reasonable tone she used to calm traffic wardens and hostile witnesses in court.

'I know you've taken against Rupert, but you're wrong. He's a . . .'

'. . . shallow snob who is just using you. If there were a competition for Mr Caring and Sharing, Rupert would be knocked out first, along with Dracula and Voldemort. He's nothing more than a corporate cowboy.'

Anthea's anger boiled over like milk. 'That's just not true! You have no idea how much he does for human rights!'

'Hey, showing up once at a charity ball for Amnesty International doesn't make him a human rights lawyer.'

'You're talking about the man I love!'

'Well, you clearly have a lot in common because *he's* in love with himself too,' Jane added, stubbornly.

It was now Anthea's turn to look at her little sister with thin-lipped disapproval. 'You're just jealous, Jane. Ever since we were teenagers, you've had enough chips on your shoulder to open a casino. Can't you be happy for me?'

'Gee, I don't know, sis. It's just that seeing two such perfect people rapt in mutual adoration makes me feel something very powerful . . . the urge to vomit! Now, if you'll excuse me, I have a husband to hunt.'

Anthea placed one hand on her sister's arm to soothe her. 'Jane, you can't just move to the other side of the world, on a whim. What about your music students? Your friends? What about your teaching job?' she asked, amazed.

'Yeah . . . my life's so busy, what with the sale at Primark and the dishwasher filter needing changing,' she answered mockingly. 'Lying in bed alone every night, I constantly remind myself that I am only one husband short of a very happy marriage!'

'But, Jane, seriously. You can't just hunt down a husband. It's not like shopping for a pair of shoes! Even Cinderella had to wait for the right glass slipper to come along.'

'You know, taking lessons in love from you is like taking ballroom dancing tips from a dinosaur. I'm going to Australia and that's all there is to it,' Jane declared in the tone of a stubborn toddler. 'And my flight is in . . .' she checked her watch '. . . five hours. I'm selling my car on the way. There's a used car lot near Heathrow.'

'Oh my God. You really are serious about this!'

Anthea seized her sister's other arm and held it tight. 'You can't go. The truth about finding a man in the Outback is that, yes, the odds may be good – but the goods will be odd. Can't you imagine how rough and tough those miners are?'

'How the hell would you know, Anthea? It's not as though you've ever been out there!' Jane yanked her arm free. 'You're just judging the place on appearances, as usual. At least there are blokes out there – and any bloke is better than no bloke,' she sighed. 'That little bit of plastic between the legs of a Barbie doll? That will be me. It will heal over.'

'Do you have any idea what kind of men live in the Outback? Criminals and misfits.' Anthea barred her sister's way to the driver's door by standing in front of it. 'People go missing out there, you know? Backpackers are murdered. In fact, I'm going to contact Extreme Sports Enthusiasts. They really should include "husband hunting in the Outback" as the ultimate risk-taking thrill.'

'You're not listening to me, Anthea! I'm sick of standing by the dips at parties, playing "Spot the Heterosexual".' Jane frowned deeply.

'If a single, hetero male does wander into our midst, he's immediately stripped down and sold off for parts. My girlfriends and I squabble over any man who still has his own teeth!' Her voice buzzed with rage, like a wasp in a jar. 'I've done everything but wear beer-flavoured lipgloss. And still nothing! For years now not one man has tried to kiss me!' She pushed past her sister and reached for the car door. 'And it's not like I'm asking for much. Just a man who can find my G-spot without a map and compass.'

'Well, when your Outback psychopath *does* kill you, just make sure you leave your brain to medical science. It's obviously never been used.'

'It's all right for you!' Jane snapped, shrilly. 'I'm tired of opening my own honey jars. And pretending to know what to do with a socket set.' Tears ran down her cheeks. 'You've never even had to change your own smoke alarm batteries, have you? You've always had a man around.'

Anthea wilted a little at the sight of Jane's tears. 'I'm sorry you haven't been lucky in love. But face facts, Jane. Australian men will bonk anything that moves and then count the legs afterwards. You must want something better than that for yourself.'

Her sister instantly stopped crying. 'You really do exceed the Daily Recommended Allowance of Smug, do you know that, Anthea? Now, move!' Sturdily built Jane flicked her delicate sister out of her way like a fly.

Anthea's nerves were now shrieking louder than the rusty hinges of an old door. 'You can't go!' It came out as a shrill command. 'What would Mum and Dad have said?'

'I don't know. But they're not here, are they? And the one thing I've learnt from losing our parents, is that life is short. You must seize the day. And I'm seizing the day like there's no tomorrow.'

'Oh, Jane, when are you going to grow up?'

'When are *you* going to grow down? You never do anything just for fun. It all has to be sensible and planned to the last detail with you.'

'Jane! Dear Jane. Answer this man's request and you're admitting you're desperate.' Anthea poked her head through the passenger window. 'Where is your dignity?'

Jane scoffed, with an expression more sour than vinegar, 'Dignity is a waste of time for

plain women. Like hair-gel for bald men. "Bye.'
She let out the clutch quickly. Anthea just had
time to jump back as the car lurched away from
the kerb.

Though she was fuming, Anthea knew this idea
of Jane's wouldn't last. Just like all her other hare-
brained schemes. She'd taught classical music
in prison. Had put on concerts for Romanian
orphans. Set up a fund in memory of their dear,
departed parents . . . Her latest fad would fizzle
out like all the rest.

Anthea took a taxi home through the leafy
calm of Hyde Park. They passed the shimmering
shop windows of Knightsbridge. For a moment
she felt relieved that their dear mother wasn't
alive to witness her sister's latest mad idea.

The cab cruised on past the quaint, cobbled
courtyards and manicured lawns of Chelsea.
Anthea wondered how anyone could hope
to find a husband in the dusty desert of the
Australian Outback. A place where the men
had only one communication skill – to whistle
or beep their car horns as they passed by. Her
poor parents would be turning in their watery
graves.

The cab finally pulled up outside her glittering Thames-side apartment. She had bought it with her inheritance, at Rupert's firm suggestion. Anthea hadn't been so sure. But he adored their modern chrome-and-glass cube sitting above the rushing tidal waters of the Thames. It had even won a prize for its design.

With its steep stairs and sharp edges, it wasn't exactly a family home. A fact which Anthea had pointed out to Rupert. But he had promised that once they married and had children, he would cash in his shares. They'd buy a big home with land in the country. Somewhere with stables and a moat and a maze, a tennis court and tree house for their many children . . . But for now, he insisted, this central location suited them perfectly.

Anthea glanced up at her apartment with pride. Then shuddered at the thought of her sister's mad trip into the windswept, dingo-infested wilds of the Aussie Outback. It would all go terribly wrong.

When Jane skulked back into London, Anthea would have to try hard not to have an attack of the 'I told you so's'. Two weeks – that was all she gave it. Two to three weeks, she thought, with a long-suffering sigh. Then she would be helping Jane put her life back on track.

She paid the taxi driver, tipping him well. She ascended the marble staircase to her flat and stepped into the arms of her perfect boyfriend.

Chapter Two

Lust At First Sight

When the wedding invitation plopped through the letterbox and on to the mat exactly one month later, Anthea fell back on to the sofa in shock. Her eyes were round as light bulbs. She made a noise like a tyre going flat. Jane . . . getting married? Anthea just couldn't believe her little sister was going to beat her down the aisle. Even if it *was* with some kind of caveman.

'A brother-in-law from the Outback. Oh, a dream come true,' Rupert drawled, peering over Anthea's shoulder at the wedding invitation. 'Jane's a classical musician, for God's sake. I didn't think she even *liked* the Great Outdoors, with all its multi-legged insects.'

'Ah, but she does like being bitten all over by desirable men . . . And the best place to find them is in the Great Outdoors. Apparently.' Anthea scrunched up the invitation and threw it in the vague direction of the waste-paper basket. 'It's the snooze alarm.'

'The what?' Rupert put down his Italian leather briefcase and unknotted his Armani tie.

'The snooze alarm's gone off on her biological clock.'

'But the silly girl's only known the man for a month. Where did she find him . . . a fiancé vending machine?' Rupert asked, retrieving the crumpled invitation from the floor and placing it neatly in the bin. 'He can only be after her money. She must have told him how much money your mum and dad left you both in their will.'

'My thoughts exactly.' Anthea handed him a glass of rich, golden wine. 'My sister's wedding vows should state, "Do you take this woman to the cleaners, from this day forth, for richer and for richer? . . . I now pronounce you Man and Mansion."'

'Looks as though this is one lucky miner who has finally struck gold,' Rupert agreed.

'I tell you what, if our parents hadn't died in that boat accident, their daughter marrying a gold-digging low life would have killed them instead.'

'I fear so, my darling. If only there were something I could do to help . . .'

Anthea still could not help feeling protective towards Jane. 'We've got to stop them. We must leave on the first plane.'

'For the Australian Outback?' Rupert shuddered. 'Yes, great place to visit – if you're a sheep. How did Jane find this . . . Aussie?' He uttered the word with distaste, as though it tasted foul and was tainting his tastebuds.

'I told you, don't you remember? She answered that ad in a newspaper, from the mayor of some mining town. He suggested ugly women should move there because the men were so desperate, they weren't too fussy.'

Rupert shook his head and gave a world-weary sigh at the stupidity of mere mortals. 'Why is it that all the other members of the animal world pair off happily, without the aid of speed dating and internet love sites? Why is it only the human of the species who needs encouragement to mate? We didn't need any help getting together, did we, darling?' He drew her towards him for a soft, lingering kiss.

For Anthea and Rupert it had been love at first sight. She'd adored him from the day she'd accidentally eaten Exhibit A. Truly. She'd been waiting in his office to discuss a legal case and had consumed the evidence – a piece of chocolate which had been left lying on his desk.

When Rupert discovered her crime, instead of throwing her off the case, he merely commented that any judge would go ahead and hold her in contempt of court – or just hold her. She had laughed with relief. To apologise, she'd bought him a drink that very night. Two days later, they were in bed together. 'I'm a human rights lawyer,' Rupert had pleaded, with mischief in his eye. 'I'm so depressed about the state of the world, I really don't think I can spend the night alone . . .'

Anthea looked up at her fiancé now as he swept one hand through his schoolboy mop of dark, floppy hair. It fell over his forehead in an endearing sweep. His smile was so bright it could act as a beacon for round-the-world yachtsmen adrift on the ocean. He flashed it at her now as he unbuttoned his shirt. He flexed his gym-toned muscles – muscles so perfect they wouldn't have looked out of place on a marble statue – and ran one hand up under her skirt while staring into her eyes. Rupert's even profile, square jaw and black-rimmed glasses always made her think of Clark Kent. By day, he looked so earnest, go-getting and smart in his pin-stripe suit. Then at night he was wild as the Caped Crusader. Removing his glasses was Rupert's signal that he was in the mood to go over to the Dark Side . . .

Anthea watched her fiancé place his specs on the coffee table and, taking her cue, snuggled herself deeper into his arms. She inhaled his familiar scent as he pulled her down on to the shag-pile rug.

Afterwards, they lay entwined on the living-room floor, as if their limbs had been deliberately styled for an advert. The waves of the incoming tide lapped at the stone wall below the apartment. Their living room, a glass cube, hung suspended over a private infinity pool. 'An infinity pool? Oh, where will it all end?' Rupert had joked the day he'd advised her to put down the deposit.

'So I'll book flights for Friday then, shall I? We have to get there before it's too late.' The

June sunlight flickered through the fronds of a potted palm. Despite the calm all around them, Anthea felt her boyfriend jerk in surprise at her question. 'Rupert?'

He winced. 'I don't think I can get away from work right now, darling. Besides which, maybe Jane's right? Single, hetero men in London are definitely harder to find than Melanie Griffith's birth certificate. Jane has at last found a man who wants to marry her. Maybe we should just let her go ahead?'

'Are you insane! The point is, if I intervene now there will be less of a mess to clean up later.'

'But face facts. If Jane were any uglier she'd need to get her mirrors insured. And maybe that mayor's got a point? What other chance do plain Janes like her have?'

'The best thing about having a sister, Rupert, is that when she doesn't know what she's doing, there is always someone else who does. Namely me. In our teens, I stopped Jane from going out with more inappropriate men than I care to remember!'

'But being single in her thirties probably does make a woman rethink her view of what is "inappropriate", Annie.'

Anthea gave her future husband a flat, measuring look. Whenever he called her 'Annie', it meant that he was trying to get out of something – taking out the rubbish, a function at her office . . . naming their wedding date. 'So, I take it you're not coming with me to Australia to save my sister?'

'Think about it, babe. If I walk into a bar in a mining town, I'll accidentally set off the Wanker City Lawyer Detector and get pulverised. Besides, I've had a tip off about the markets. I think the time is nearly right to sell my shares . . .'

Anthea's eyes lit up. 'Really?' Selling his shares was Rupert's coded way of saying that he was finally ready to marry her, settle down and have children.

He squeezed her closer to him. 'I think the time is right, don't you?' he said, in a voice dripping with honey, 'to make the ultimate long-term investment . . .'

'Oh, sweetheart, I do, I really do.' She kissed him deeply.

'I'm sure you'll do what's best for that sad sis of yours.' Rupert was nodding his head sympathetically, but his mind was somewhere else. He was thinking about the stock market, his current case . . . Anthea was too excited by the prospect of her own wedding arrangements to be annoyed by his distracted manner.

'Besides, you'll be back in no time.' There was a tone of smug certainty in his voice. 'Jane's just trying to get one up on you. There probably is no fiancé.' Then he snatched the invitation out of the bin where he'd tossed it earlier. 'She's calling him Bill Jackman, eh?' Rupert sounded amused. 'Well, even if he does exist, one peep at your sister naked and it will all be over.'

Anthea felt a flicker of irritation. Yes, Jane was annoying but she was still family. 'My sister's not that bad-looking, Rupert.'

'I know . . . I know. I'm sorry. It's just that she will insist on stuffing herself with fast food. She should take a heavily pregnant woman with her everywhere she goes, just to make her look slimmer.'

Although tempted to laugh, Anthea clicked her tongue in disapproval.

Rupert stroked her thigh. '*You* won the genetic lottery though, didn't you? Sometimes I can't believe you're not adopted. And I can't wait to make you my wife. Just think of the beautiful children we'll produce.'

Anthea smiled indulgently at her husband-to-be and nestled securely in the crook of his arm, like a baby.

Chapter Three

Hate At First Sight

When Anthea first saw the Outback town near to which her sister intended to make her home, it was hate at first sight. It was hard to say what she hated most about it. Was it the heat? The air was so dry the trees were positively whistling for dogs, and the chickens were laying hard-boiled eggs.

Or was it maybe the 'super pit'? The open-cut mine looked as vast and deep as the Grand Canyon. Massive trucks, each wheel the size of a seaside bungalow, toiled up and down its raw, red slopes – day in, day out.

No, the sewage pit had to be worse. It sent up an unspeakable stench in the sun and attracted a black fog of flies. Worse even than that was the Aboriginal settlement. There were rows of windowless dormitories where she was appalled to discover that whole families lived. These identical cement structures were built between the two pits – the sewage and the super.

But surely the worst aspect of Broken Ridge mining town was the casual racism. 'What did Jesus say to the Abos when he was up on the cross?' her cab driver bantered on the way there. She tried not to stare at his vast buttocks spilling over the bucket seat. 'Don't do anything till I get back!'

Anthea had recoiled in horror. But even more unnerving than the casual racism were the many bars and brothels she saw. Her driver had bragged that they were all open '24/7' to accommodate the men on shift work. 'They offer around the cock service,' he guffawed, running his bitten nails through his thinning hair. 'Those girls are working away at, well, beaver pitch!'

Anthea crossed her legs primly in the back of his dusty cab and pursed her mouth in disgust. What on earth had her irresponsible, erratic sister got herself into *this* time?

The driver gunned the taxi past what he called the 'starting stalls'. These turned out to be a row of corrugated tin cubicles in which women sat, half-naked and in provocative poses, awaiting customers. It was like a rustic, rusty, rundown Aussie version of Amsterdam's red light district. Her driver unwound his window. He slowed down and called out to the girls, 'Show us yer pink bits.'

Anthea was horrified. 'My goodness, I just can't imagine why there's a shortage of eligible women here,' she said sarcastically.

'It's a nightmare,' her driver confirmed, missing her joke. 'The whole town's full of horny miners and farmers, bustin' for the company of a decent sheila.'

'So, what are you looking for in a female companion?' Anthea probed.

'You just gotta be breathing,' came his romantic reply.

Anthea was seriously regretting her decision to come to the Outback. Things had not got off to a good start. Jane had rung her mobile and left a message to say that two of her music students had been late. Could Anthea get a taxi into town? She was to wait at a pub called, rather disturbingly, The Lucky Shag. In a bar there called, even more ominously, Skimpy's. Jane and her fiancé Jacko would meet her.

The driver dropped Anthea beneath the neon

'Lucky Shag' sign. It fizzed pointlessly beneath the searing sun. As she fished around in her purse, the driver promised her a free t-shirt if she had a drink in all of the town's forty bars. She supposed there were also matching underpants to go with the t-shirts, as a reward for quenching one's sexual thirst at every brothel. But she knew better than to make any comment which might lead him on. Even without encouragement, he was being persistent. He leant out of the taxi window to tuck his card into her bra strap. 'The bar you want's in that door. Though you're a bit overdressed for Skimpy's!' he laughed. 'Call me any time on this number, sugar tits.' He leered at her, before revving away.

'And you wonder why you're single?' she seethed under her breath, in a fug of exhaust fumes.

The relentless blue sky screeched down at her. The whole town seemed to bray like a drunken bloke laughing too loudly at a party. Spending time in such a bar was second on Anthea's List of Least Favourite Things to do . . . right after chopping off her own leg with nail scissors.

Anthea walked into the saloon as though she already wanted to leave. It was the kind of bar where even the water is watered down. The clamour of male voices which greeted her sounded like a hippo giving birth. Anthea balanced on the edge of a sticky stool. Oh, how she wished she had mastered the art of levitation. Or else knew how to turn herself into a human hovercraft. She checked her watch and jiggled her foot with irritation.

As her eyes adjusted to the gloom, she understood the bar's name. The barmaids at Skimpy's were wearing the skimpiest underwear imaginable. They were the opposite of icebergs – ninety per cent of them was visible. The customer on Anthea's right flipped a two-dollar coin, slapped it down on the bar and called 'heads'.

'I won!' he exclaimed to the nearest barmaid. Since he'd won the toss, the bored girl then lifted her bra and casually flashed her bare breasts at him. Another man who was wearing a shirt which read 'I got crabs at Big Dick's' had lost his toss. So the barmaid got to keep his coin and what remained of her modesty. Anthea's spirits fell even further. It was clear that the only support a woman got in this town was from her Wonderbra.

She ordered a mineral water, checking the glass for grime before putting it to her lips. Despair filled her heart. What on earth was her sister doing in this Godforsaken cesspit?

The answer to that question arrived on cue. Dear God, don't let that be him, Anthea thought as he gangled in the doorway, all legs and elbows. She turned back to the bar but soon felt the man's gaze like hot breath on the nape of her neck. The sound of his boots rang out on the bare wooden floorboards as he strode towards her.

In long, sliding, unhurried vowels, the object of her sister's affections said, 'You must be Anne.'

'. . . *thea* . . .' She squeezed as much emphasis into the correction as was humanly possible. 'Anthea.'

He took off his cowboy hat to reveal straggly black hair. 'I'm Jacko.'

Narrowing her eyes with keen interest, Anthea surveyed her potential brother-in-law. Bill Jackman was the opposite of what was usually required of a romantic hero. Mid-forties, in weathered riding boots and faded jeans, he was too tall, at about six foot four. His shirt stuck to him like a khaki skin, revealing a powerfully built body. But the muscular, mahogany-tanned flesh was matted with thick hair. Tufts of it sprouted from the open V of his shirt.

He had the kind of face you wouldn't wish on a bull terrier – the kind you associate with crime scene programmes. It was as if his face had been carved by a trainee sculptor. Individually, the features were attractive, but together they didn't work. Acne scars pitted his cheeks. Stubble worked through the cratered surface around his flattened nostrils. Anthea wondered whether his crushed nose was the original edition or had been broken – and how many men he'd hospitalised in the fight.

'Where's my sister?' she asked, with alarm. Murdered, no doubt, and being minced up for dog food meat right this very minute . . . Hideous visions crowded her muddled brain.

'Janey's running late. What with her teaching, the wedding plans and preparing your welcome feast . . . the poor girl's run off her pretty little feet. My property's a good hour out of town. Knowing my Janey, she probably secretly thought it would be a good way for us to spend some time together. So we can really get to know each other.'

Anthea already had a good idea who Bill Jackman was – the kind of misfit Jerry Springer would base an entire show around. She gave a shiver of horror at the thought of being alone with him and made a hasty phone call to her sister's mobile.

'Anthea! How exciting that you're actually here.' Her little sister's vowels had already flattened slightly, with her voice taking on an Australian twang. Anthea heard this, with disapproval. 'Where are you now?'

'Oh, obviously at my Joy And Rapture Seminar,' she snapped. 'I've flown half way around the world to see you. Yet you couldn't be bothered to pick me up?'

'Calm down. It'll be good for Jacko to drive you out to the homestead. It will give you a chance to bond.'

'If I don't kill him first. Why do women always make the mistake of thinking that if they marry an awful man, they can change him? The only time you can ever change a male of the species, Jane, is out of a nappy as a baby.'

Jane sighed. The initial excitement of hearing her sister drained out of her voice. 'Make an effort for once in your life, will you? After all, he will be your brother-in-law in a month's time.'

'Not if I can help it,' Anthea said to her beer mat as she rang off.

She pocketed her phone then turned to study her sister's beau. 'So, apparently you've decided to *marry* . . .' Anthea said the word with utter contempt '. . . my beloved sister, after only knowing her for three or so weeks. I'm sure you can understand why this makes me uneasy. I mean, we know nothing about you.' She selected 'patronising' from her range of facial expressions. 'Do you have any convictions?'

Jacko gave a playful smirk. 'Nope . . . but you obviously do. That all men are bastards for one.'

'No,' she said crossly. 'I mean *prior* convictions.'

'Yeah, that all the blokes you met *prior* to your fiancé are bastards too. He's a lawyer, right? Your fiancé?' Jacko picked up her suitcase. 'Must be such a fun bloke.' He winked at her. 'Does he send his shirts out to be stuffed?'

Anthea looked at her future brother-in-law with the kind of expression you'd give an incontinent nudist who had just relieved himself on your bridal dress.

43

'Shall we go?' He extended one hand to help her down from the bar stool.

She was reluctant to take it, not having had a rabies shot. She clambered down from the bar stool unaided and flounced outside. What she saw next stopped her dead in her tracks.

Chapter Four

Eye Sore

Dear God, she thought. Don't let that be his car. But sure enough, Jacko was opening the door of the battered utility truck before her. Actually Anthea wasn't sure if it was a truck or the *Starship Enterprise*, as it sported enough antennae to get it to Jupiter and back. 'Mr Jackman, you don't expect me to get into *that*, do you?'

'Sorry, ma'am. Not the limousine you're used to, I know. But a four-wheel-drive is safer out here.'

'Mr Jackman, you understand my reluctance, I take it. And why I need to ask you a few things first. I hope you don't mind . . .' she eyed his rusty vehicle with disdain '. . . but what exactly are your prospects?'

Jacko let out a snort of laughter. 'I'm a miner, love. I have prospects all over the bloody place!'

He swung her small leopardskin suitcase into the back of the utility truck. It looked completely out of place alongside tools, tarpaulins and a tethered motorbike. As out of place as she did. 'But I do an honest day's work. Not like those desk-jockey knobs and total tossbags in town.'

Anthea's eyebrows shot up her forehead. Ignoring his helpful hand once more, she hauled herself into the passenger seat and arranged the hem of her linen dress around her knees. In the heat, her clothes and hair had wilted like week-old lettuce. But both were positively buoyant compared to her spirits. Jacko vaulted into the driver's seat and thrust the key into the ignition.

'It's only natural that I feel protective towards my little sister,' Anthea explained, her expression pinched. 'As you no doubt know, we lost our parents two years ago in a horrific boating accident. Since then I've tried to take care of Jane. But she is extremely impulsive . . .'

'Don't you ever act on impulse, Anne-*thea*?' Jacko laughed. He laced his fingers behind his neck and flexed his massive arm muscles in a casual stretch before pulling away from the pavement. 'Thinking's overrated, if yer ask me,' he said.

'Human beings are not just a mass of impulses, Mr Jackman. It's only natural that I should ask exactly what your *intentions* are towards my sister,' she said, even though she realized she was sounding just like a starchy old aunt in a Victorian novel.

'I intend to make your sister very happy.' Jacko gave her another cheeky wink. He then drove at a leisurely pace down the wide red dirt road, waving to passersby and occasionally hooting his horn in greeting. 'Very, very happy.'

'Oh, yes? And how exactly do you plan to do that?' Anthea's voice was clipped. 'You're taking her away from her friends, her job, her home, her hemisphere. And for what? To make her live *here*?' She gestured at the ramshackle town huddled around the gaping mine. 'In this racist, sexist hellhole.'

Jacko cast an amused glance over Anthea and then, to her surprise, laughed right out loud. 'Sure, the blokes around here are rough. But at least what you see is what you get. Those city blokes only call themselves "male feminists" in the hope of getting a more intelligent bonk.'

The streets thinned out fast. They were churning out of town now through scorched countryside. A recent bush fire had left the black skeletons of trees dotted across the landscape. The utility truck lurched into gravelled hollows, its wheels noisily throwing up dirt and gravel.

'What else can I make of a town which calls the seam of gold you mine "The Body"? What kind of image does that conjure up? A geological Elle Macpherson, crawling with men,' Anthea protested.

'But in a town with one female to every fifty blokes, it's surely the women who are "sitting on a goldmine".' Jacko gave a rich chuckle at his own joke.

Anthea shot him a disapproving look. 'Yes, your mayor has made that perfectly clear,' she replied. 'But if you ask me, it's obscene – luring plain, vulnerable women out here to Broken Ridge on the pretext of offering them love. When in reality you men just can't be bothered to pay for a prostitute.'

Jacko gave her a polite but sullen look. 'Steady on, old girl. We're not that bad. Contrary to the stereotype, we country blokes don't have sex with just anything with a hole and a heartbeat . . . and then count the legs afterwards. Company, that's what we crave . . . No, it's the city fellas you've got to worry about. They've got you women starving yourselves and cutting your faces to stay young and beautiful. Jane reckons if your boyfriend . . . what's that city slicker's name again?'

'Rupert. If you must know. Rupert Cavendish.'

'Well, she reckons that if your Rupert told you to eat only pedicure shavings for a more lively complexion, you'd damn' well do it. Skin has only one function, yer know, Anthea. To stop your insides from slopping out all over the place . . . But it'll no doubt take you two thousand diets and twenty-eight surgical procedures to realise that you'd be much more beautiful if you read a book now and then. Besides a legal textbook that is. Jane . . . now, *there's* a reader for you,' he concluded, fondly.

This unexpected speech left Anthea shaking all over, like a dog swarmed by bees. Okay, the miner had better communication skills than she'd anticipated, but how dare he talk to her that way? Stalling for time, she extracted her lipstick from the pocket of her dress and reapplied a crimson layer. She forced a smile, but it was sharp as a razor.

'The truth is, Mr Jackman, I don't need to be

informed of my sister's many and wonderful qualities. Those I know about already. It's just totally beyond me what she sees in *you*. Although I'm sure there's nothing wrong with you that an exorcism couldn't fix,' she said, cruelly.

'Is that right?' Jacko dodged a lump of rotting road kill. 'But really, am I that unattractive?' he joked. 'At the mine, you can see in at the window of my shower from the women's changing rooms. I've been meaning to get a blind but, hey, why spoil their view?' He laughed encouragingly.

Anthea refused to be amused. She bestowed on him the kind of icy look which could have got her the part of an extra in a Dracula movie. Jacko's smile died on his lips. But not, as Anthea thought, because of her snooty response. The truck was rounding a bend in the road at speed. And there, right in their path, lay a fallen tree. Jacko slammed on the brakes. The truck corkscrewed to a halt.

Anthea lurched forward. She was then snapped back by her seat belt. The massive, charred gum tree lay right across the track. Weakened by the recent fire, it had toppled from the shallow ridge above the left-hand side of the road. The way ahead was totally blocked by a snarled wall of branches, leaves and blackened trunk.

Jacko slowly steered to the right side of the road and peered out of the window. The hill pitched down steeply into a tangle of dense scrub.

'Damn,' he announced. 'No way round.'

'Can't you call someone to come and clear it?'

Jacko laughed. 'We're on bush time here, love. Nobody does anything in a hurry.'

'Except fall in "love", apparently,' Anthea responded, sarcastically.

Jacko knew that a comment like that should be stepped around as carefully as a dozing crocodile. 'Could be hours before they clear this lot,' he said. 'Jane's dinner will be ruined . . . Don't worry, I know a back road. Old fire trail. Don't want to miss out on our tucker. Your sister's a hell of a cook as you know.'

'Actually I know no such thing. Are we talking about the same person?' Anthea was growing tired of hearing about all of her sister's talents. She had little doubt that Jacko was really interested in just one recipe. The recipe for success that he could attain using Jane's inheritance.

Jacko swung the truck around, retraced their route for a mile or so, then lurched off on to a red dirt track. What would probably be classified as a traffic hazard anywhere else in the civilised world, Jacko saw as an actual road. The truck lurched and catapulted its way up the hill. It was a car journey which threatened to shake the fillings out of their teeth.

As the red earth gave way to rock, Anthea began to worry that she was being abducted. But once they crested the ridge and nose-dived down the other side, she could see that they were indeed heading in the same direction as the main road far below.

'Anyway,' Jacko picked up on his previous theme, 'that's what I love about your sister. She doesn't judge a book, or in my case a bloke, by the cover. Besides which, do you know why it's better to go out with a rough and ready, ugly bloke? Because we're so damn' grateful. Which makes us so much less demanding . . . I get down on bended knee and thank Jane for coming into my life, every damn' day. I worship that woman. I suppose your legal eagle fella just expects you to worship the water he walks on',

Jacko laughed as the utility truck moaned its way up an incline.

Anthea was enraged once more. How dare he keep talking to her this way? They'd only just met and here he was, making inappropriate remarks about her boyfriend. She reeled around to face him. But as the car laboured up the rough ridge, the barrage of barbed replies on the tip of her tongue were abruptly silenced. A blur of feathers filled the screen. Anthea recoiled with fear, a scream in her blood. Jacko spun the wheel.

The truck slid sideways. It hit something solid and rolled over. The windscreen cracked on impact then shattered. As she tumbled over and over in the cabin of the truck, terror exploded on to the screen of her eyelids. There was a smell of burning rubber followed by the deafening roar of crumpling metal. The earth and sky blurred, and then the world imploded. Anthea was aware of smashing glass, a tinkling sound like waves on shingle, and then the world went black.

Chapter Five

If Looks Could Kill – Hate At First *Slight*

Anthea felt herself clawing her way back to consciousness. Patterns of light flickered across her closed eyelids. She opened her eyes to find she was lying on a blanket on some soft sand, her whole body coated in dust. The sting of blood was in her nostrils. Each ragged breath she took felt like inhaling fire, but the elation of still being alive engulfed her.

'What . . . What happened?' she stuttered.

'Emu. Big bugger too. A male. Bounded into our path. Truck's rooted – totally wrecked.'

A belch of petrol alerted her to the fate of the demolished truck, lying upside down in what appeared to be a giant ditch beside them. The aftershock rippled through her body and a bubble of hysteria rose in her chest.

'An emu? Aren't you supposed to know about these things? How could you just drive casually off the beaten track while there are giant creatures like that bounding about? Not only do you look as thick as a plank, you're even less intelligent.'

'I've got 'roo bars on the front of the truck,' Jacko protested. 'But I wasn't counting on the death wish of our feathered friend. Emus are so bloody stupid. He saw the car and ran right into it. Worse than a 'roo, too, 'cause its body mass is just at window level. Which is why the glass smashed to smithereens . . .'

'Suicidal emus . . . You see! Even the wildlife are depressed, living out here.' Anthea's voice had risen two octaves with terror.

Jacko moved closer, squatted down and scrutinised her. 'You've been out for the count for yonks. Are you okay?' She now noted that, despite his surface calm, Jacko's skin had gone the colour of a cold roast.

Still shell-shocked, Anthea did a quick check of her limbs then wiggled her toes and swivelled her neck. There didn't seem to be any serious pain. When she nodded that she was indeed okay, Jacko's smile broke across his face like a wave over a beach.

'Well, that's a bloody relief. Don't know what Jane would have done to me if I'd accidentally maimed her only sister. Reckon she'd be using my testicles for earrings.'

Anthea winced at the crudeness of his language. 'Have you called an ambulance?'

'Phone's smashed. And yours is out of range. I checked it.'

'Oh, no! Oh my God,' she squeaked. 'Then what are we going to do?' Panic gripped her.

Jacko, on the other hand, didn't seem to be remotely stressed. 'I dunno. Eat dinner?' He tilted his head towards some point beyond her shoulder. 'He's roasting nicely in the embers. At least we can have our revenge on that big stupid bird. Emu kebab.'

Anthea craned her neck in the direction he was pointing. A little fire was burning in a make-shift rocky hearth. Jacko got up and went over to poke at the smouldering pile. He kicked away the ashes and cut into the charred bird with a penknife. A tangy roasting aroma filled Anthea's nostrils and whetted her appetite. He offered her some cooked white meat, skewered on the end of his penknife. But she resolutely shook her head.

'Road kill? You seriously expect me to eat

road kill? Tell me, are you just visiting from pre-historic times? Or are you actually planning to live here for good?'

'Bloody handy, eh, that we got hit by some-thing edible? And how lucky was it that we rolled into a riverbed? And for the river to be dry? Talk about a soft landing.'

'Lucky? You think this is lucky? . . . Well, at least you've brought religion into my life, Mr Jackman. I now really do know what it's like to be in hell. We could die out here!'

Jacko raised one furry brow in amusement. 'Well, *I* won't. But *you* could. You're too damn' scrawny. I could play your spine like a xylophone. A woman needs a bit of meat on her bones. Like my Janey.'

Anthea was offended. 'Unlike my sister, I take pride in my appearance.'

Jacko laughed in her face. 'So tell me, how many years of yoga does it take to be able to kiss your own ass like that? Have you actually *looked* in a mirror lately, woman? You're so thin, your pyjamas must have only *one* stripe.'

Anthea felt a mixture of fury and despair well up in her. A sob erupted from her and her face crumpled.

'Hey, come on now. Don't have a meltdown,' Jacko said in a more comforting voice. 'Now the fire's lit, we'll be sticking out like a dog's balls. A spotter plane will find us, easy. Once Jane realises that we're overdue, she'll call the cops. All the locals are bound to come looking for us. Pilots . . . well, they're civil contractors, really, the guys who drop the miners back and forth from the city . . . they fly by all the time. She'll be right. Don't you worry.'

'Worry! Of course I'm worried. Or do you think I always gnaw my nails right up to my elbows? I need some water,' she demanded.

Jacko rummaged around in his Gore-Tex backpack and handed her a water bottle. 'I've got painkillers too,' he offered.

'Just water,' Anthea said crisply. She didn't want to risk taking anything. Not when she was marooned in the Outback with an obvious maniac. She needed to keep her wits about her. Anthea took a swig of water then poured some on to her hands.

'Oy!' Jacko snatched back the bottle. 'What the hell do you think you're doing? That water's for drinking only. We're in the middle of the desert, in case you hadn't noticed,' he yelled. 'You think *I'm* thick? Jesus. If brains were elastic, yours couldn't make a garter for a canary.'

'But I'm covered in red dust,' Anthea whined.

'Tough. Unless you want me to lick you clean,' he laughed.

Anthea prickled with disgust at his suggestion. 'Don't be revolting.'

'Relax. I'm only joking. Jeez, I'm beginning to think you wouldn't know a joke if it jumped up and bit you on the bum.'

'But didn't you say we're in a creek bed?'

'Yes, a dry creek bed . . . About as dry as your bloody personality,' he said under his breath.

'What? What did you say?' she fumed. 'I heard that!'

Jacko was back at the fire now, poking around in the ashes. Anthea watched him cut off another huge hunk of charred emu with his penknife. He thrust some white meat in her direction on the end of the blade.

Anthea recoiled once more.

Jacko shook his head. 'Your stomach must think that your throat's been cut. Okay, it's not exactly cock-a-leekie-dick-in-the-spotted-hole or whatever the hell it is you people eat in England. But it's good bush tucker.'

As he chewed her share, Jacko eyed her thoughtfully. 'Look, you're probably in shock. That's why you're acting as though you've got kangaroos in your top paddock.' He tapped his head, by way of explanation. 'But don't sweat it. Why don't you just look on the whole adventure as a spur-of the-moment camping trip? You can experience first hand what it's like to get back to the land.'

'Camping doesn't make me want to get back to the land. It makes me want to get back to a five-star hotel suite for a bubble bath.'

'But just look around you,' Jacko insisted. 'The birdsong, the wind whispering in the gum trees, the landscape dotted with 'roos . . .'

'Men may find it romantic to sleep rough and live off the land, cooking on a campfire. To most women it just describes fleeing the Japanese army in the Second World War through the jungles of Borneo.'

Jacko let out a loud bark of a laugh. 'Jane said just the same thing to me the other day. She reckons the true definition of a campsite is an insect-infested area, enclosing nostalgic, competitive men and pissed off, freezing cold women who are secretly planning a mass exodus to the nearest shopping mall.'

'Or concert hall,' Anthea added, pointedly. 'Doesn't that illustrate just how ill-suited you are? This is why I'm so worried about your future together. Think it through, Mr Jackman. You're a bushman. Jane's natural habitat is the opera house. She should be with the kind of man who went to a famous college. Like Rupert did.' The thought of him was like a warm embrace. 'The sort of man who will one day cure cancer. Or invent something astonishing. And you . . . well . . .' Anthea cast a scornful glance at her companion.

Jacko curled his lip at her superior tone. 'I have my talents,' was all he said.

'Like what? Driving a car off the road and nearly killing your passenger?'

'Like living off the land. Personally, I can't think of a more important skill.'

'Oh my God. What's that noise?' Anthea replied. 'Oh, I know. It's the sound of millions of women laughing themselves to death . . . I mean, how ridiculous. We've had centuries of civilisation. We don't need to live off the land any more.'

'Yeah. Your type just live off your rich, successful husbands.'

Now it was Anthea's turn to take offence. 'I don't live off Rupert! I am an independent career woman, I'll have you know.' She felt perplexed. Surely Jane's inheritance was the only reason he was marrying her sister. And yet he was acting as though he didn't know anything about the money.

'I'm a survivor. Once, when I was in the army, I came within a whisker of being paralysed in a free fall from a helicopter. I had to bite the head off a snake to survive. I slept inside a slaughtered camel to stave off hypothermia in the desert. Out here, your precious Rupert would be about as useful as a . . .' Jacko cast around for the right words '. . . as an ashtray on a motorbike.' He looked lovingly at his Harley-Davidson, half buried but still intact under the upside down truck.

'Oh, really? Well, I'd love to see how you'd survive in the urban jungle. Man versus Wilderness is one thing. But what about Man versus Child Minding?' Anthea ranted. 'Yes, you've demonstrated survival skills in one of the world's most desolate regions . . . But can you survive the brutal realities of marriage? The fights over housework and food shopping? The school run? The perils of Parent Teacher Night?'

Anthea took a deep breath, and continued. 'Yes, you've climbed great mountains, but what about social climbing? Have you got a head for heights? How will you cope with Jane's smart musician friends? Okay, you survived a free fall jump from a helicopter. But what about the free fall when your babysitter cancels and the kids come down with flu and Jane's playing in the city at a concert? How will you cope then, eh?'

'Do you know what? You should give up the law and get a job as a life saver in a sewage plant 'cause you talk such shit. You've just dismissed all Aussie blokes as a bunch of retarded rednecks. But you know nothing about us. You know what? Maybe it's kind of a good thing that the truck rolled and we have this enforced time together. So you can get to know me better.'

'A good thing? Oh, yes, I'm just so glad I left behind my lovely soft mattress and beautiful boyfriend in London, to be nearly crushed to death by a deranged emu, forced to eat road kill, and marooned in the middle of the desert. Not to mention becoming an-all-you-can-eat diner for sand flies the size of Sumo wrestlers!' She swatted angrily at a buzzing insect.

If Jacko could have swatted *her*, he would have. 'So tell me, Anthea, have you always been such a pain in the ass or do you take lessons?'

'Obviously Jane is having some kind of mental breakdown. Otherwise why would she come out here?' Anthea looked around her at the unfamiliar, harsh landscape and shuddered.

'She came here 'cause the place is full of Real Men. I suppose your poncey Rupert can only get aroused if you touch him on the gonads with a velvet opera glove. Maybe *you'll* even fall for a real bloke out here. Maybe I can arrange it. So, tell me, exactly what kind of Aussie fella would you like to meet?'

'One who is doused in petrol and has a stake driven through his heart, preferably,' Anthea muttered.

'Jeez,' he said, amazed. 'You are a woman who speaks her mind, aren't you?'

'That's because I have one,' she retorted. 'You're obviously only attracted to my sister because of the novelty of being with a woman you don't have to inflate.'

Jacko's body went as taut as an archer's bow.

Anthea drew back. She was frightened she'd finally pushed him too far. He leapt to his feet. Anthea shrank back even more. But his eyes were fixed on something behind her. With a jerk, he yanked her upright.

'Do you mind? Ouch! Don't touch me. That hurts.'

'Move!'

'Why?'

Jacko thrust her roughly towards the river-bank. 'Tsunami.'

'What!'

'Get out of the creek. Quick!'

'Don't be ridiculous. We're hundreds of miles from the sea. We're . . .'

Movement caught Anthea's eye. She glanced over her shoulder to see a wall of water, five feet high, surging down the dry creek bed behind them. It moved quickly and quietly, churning up the red earth before it.

Jacko bounded up the bank in five giant steps. But Anthea just stood stock still, spellbound by the sight of all that muddy water racing towards her. Part of her thought it must be a mirage . . . Until the wave hit her chest. She lost her balance, buckled at the knees and slid into the torrent.

Jacko waded back in and grabbed her. Water gushed around their bodies, trying to drag them downstream. Jacko hauled her towards the bank.

'Inland tsunami. Means there's been a storm a hundred miles away. Now, move. There'll be even more water coming.'

Anthea could see that the flood was getting deeper. It was also getting faster. The riverbed where their truck had turned over was wide. The mangled vehicle groaned and lurched forward in the current. She watched in astonishment as the metal carcass was churned downstream and out of sight.

'My Harley!' Jacko cried, as the beloved big bike also faded from view.

But there was no time for the big man to mourn. The current was getting stronger. When they had finally waded into the shallows, a surge of relief went through Anthea. But just when she thought she'd reached safety, Jacko took hold of her and pushed her down again into the swirling water. A panicked thought pierced her mind. Mother Nature had presented the maniac with a perfect opportunity to be rid of his fiancée's prying sister. He could really drown his sorrows – if he held her head under for long enough. Once she was dead, he could get his hands on Jane's money with no questions asked. She kicked out at Jacko and broke free of him. In her urgency to get away, she stumbled backwards and went under.

As the dark, muddy flood heaved around her, she thrashed about trying to keep her head above water. The turbulent undercurrent had her somersaulting crazily. Confused, Anthea couldn't find the way up. Gasping for air but only swallowing water, her mind starting floating in a way that her body was not. Maybe I'm dreaming? she thought . . . But if so, then where was George Clooney and why wasn't she naked?

Two strong arms encircled her body. She came up out of the murky whirlpool, coughing. Her nose streamed. The rational world seemed to be spinning completely out of its orbit.

Jacko had swum downstream after her. Dragging her towards shore, he hooked one arm over a drooping tree branch. The other remained clamped around Anthea. Both of them were chest-deep in the choppy water. The river rushed past, jerking her violently this way and that. 'Why the hell did you push me down into the water?' she spluttered. 'Why save me, then drown me? You obviously took an IQ test and failed,' she ranted. Terrified as she was, her only thought was to give the man a good tongue lashing. 'If ignorance is bliss, then you must be permanently on cloud nine . . .'

Anthea's insults trailed off because Jacko was pointing at something. She followed his finger to see what could only be described as a small dinosaur thrashing towards them at speed. As it was swept along on the heaving tide, it struck out with its claws, slashing at floating debris.

'Goanna. Claws like razors. Can rip you open. They climb up the tallest thing they can see. Which, in this creek, is you and me. Would cut you open like a tin can. That's why I had to get you back down into the drink,' Jacko explained. The giant lizard thrashed past on powerful legs, its head twisting this way and that in fright.

Unsure whether her travel insurance covered gaping chest wounds from prehistoric lizards, Anthea gripped hold of Jacko. Having totally rejected the man earlier, she now clung to him like nylon worn in a heat wave. As soon as the goanna had hurtled downstream, Jacko placed his hands on Anthea's backside and propelled her up the bank.

She scrambled her way up the slope then lay there panting, her body twisted, arms flung wide, busily converting to religion. There are many reasons for sudden religious conversion. A particularly good one is finding yourself swept up in an inland tsunami.

Chapter Six

Seeing Is Disbelieving

Jacko vaulted up the bank without losing a breath. 'Shit. My backpack's gone,' he exclaimed. 'With both our phones in it.' Noticing Anthea's pale face, he added, 'Look on the bright side. With no phones, we get to spend even more time with each other!'

She blinked up at him, water still streaming from her nose. Anthea was used to being in total control. She was aware that tears were welling up in her eyes. Desperate to hide how shaken up she felt, she lashed out verbally. 'I'm looking forward to spending more time with you about as much as I'm looking forward to my own execution by firing squad . . . A car crash, an inland tsunami, a wild goanna . . . This is a prank, isn't it? We're being secretly filmed for some reality TV show, aren't we?' she said, still struggling to take in all that had happened.

But Jacko's attention was elsewhere. He was looking up at the jaundiced clouds on the horizon. They threatened rain. And yet, above them, the sky was clear. But there was something odd in the air. Anthea's hair went static suddenly. It frizzed and stood on end. The slight fuzz on her arms was also standing to attention.

'Oh, dear God. What's going on *now*?' she asked, alarmed.

'Static electricity. The air's so parched, even the bloody ions are dry.'

Anthea studied the skyline. The weather seemed as wild as a teenager's mood. In the distance she could see sunshine, showers, an electrical storm, hailstones and rainbows all at once. She didn't like it. To unnerve her even more, a flock of white cockatoos erupted from a tree perched atop the hill behind them. Anthea reeled around to see the birds fly screeching into the air. It was as though someone had thrown a huge handful of confetti into the heavens. And then, as if things couldn't get any more surreal, the tree in which the cockatoos had been nesting burst into flames.

'Well, I'll be blowed!' Jacko marvelled. 'A bolt

from the blue. I've never seen that before. Quite an awesome event.'

'A bolt from the what?'

'A lightning strike. Without a storm. A bolt from the blue . . . Pretty much like your sister coming into my life when I least expected it.' He smiled.

Before Anthea had time to reply to his comment, Jacko lunged at her. He started ripping at the row of buttons running down the front of her dress.

'What the hell do you think you're doing? Get off me, you pervert . . .' She slapped at his hands. 'Unless you'd prefer to be separated from your scrotum.'

'Get your bra off!' he commanded.

Anthea dug her nails into the skin of his forearm. 'Get away from me!' Panic rose in her chest. She kicked out in the direction of his groin. 'Or you'll be auditioning for the Vienna Boys' Choir. I am not kidding.'

'Underwire.'

'What?'

'Underwire. In your bra. If lightning strikes again, it could electrocute you.'

Jacko ruched her dress up at the back. In

one deft movement, he reached up, unhooked her bra and slipped the straps down over her shoulders. He then groped up the front of her frock and pulled the lacy white bra free, flinging it into the raging river.

Anthea felt relieved that he wasn't groping her, but also indignant at his total control. She reacted the only way she knew how, with barbed banter. 'I don't care if I get electrocuted. Just don't come near me again! You Outback blokes may be starved for female affection but, believe me, seeing you naked would almost certainly turn me into a lesbian.'

A sound like a gunshot cracked through the air, making her jump. 'What is it *now*?' she wailed.

'Gum nuts. It's the eucalyptus oil in the trees. Makes them explode. The tinder's so dry the whole place could go up in smoke in an instant.' Jacko licked his finger and held it aloft. 'But we're okay. Don't worry. The wind's not blowing in this direction.'

No sooner had he finished speaking than the bush on the hill above them ignited. Gum nuts started exploding everywhere like grenades. As a wall of heat rose up, birds bickered and raced for safety. The crows wailed like alley cats. A few moments later it was like a scene from a biblical plague. Snakes, lizards, birds, kangaroos, wallabies and wombats all started twisting, writhing, bounding and scrabbling down the side of the hill.

'The wind will push the fire east, if we're lucky.'

'Lucky! Luck has nothing to do with it! Planning. That's what's missing here. Planning is a vital component of any trip . . . Just ask Scott of the Antarctic,' she said hysterically.

'Shut up,' Jacko barked.

'Don't tell me to shut up.' She glared at him resentfully. Okay, he might have saved her life once or twice in the past hour, but the man really was insufferable. 'Why is it that every time you talk, I get an overwhelming urge to be alone . . .'

'Plane!' he yelled.

Jacko and Anthea lifted their arms into the air simultaneously, as though doing an aerobics class.

Jacko ripped off his white shirt. He ran to the highest point that wasn't ablaze and started waving the shirt wildly above his head. Anthea couldn't help but notice his taut abdomen and muscular physique. He was surprisingly agile and fit for a man his age.

'How will we know if the pilot's seen us!' she cried.

'He'll dip one wing.'

Jacko kept waving frantically. Anthea now joined him, moving her arms like the sails of a windmill. Her hopes had risen nearly as high as the small silver plane.

'Dip, you bastard. Dip!' Jacko urged.

She squinted against the sun to follow the plane's progress through the big, broad sky. Jacko kept jumping up and down and waving his improvised flag. But no matter how hard she willed the pilot to see them, the plane veered left and moved away.

'Bugger it. The pilot's too busy getting away from the storm to notice us . . .' Jacko turned his attention back towards the blazing bush. He then went so rigid Anthea thought he'd been shot. She watched as he came barrelling back down the slope towards her, his expression fierce. 'Wind's changed.'

Anthea noted that the noise level had gone up around her. Gone were the sounds like hand grenades. The noise now resembled cannon fire. She turned to see the limbs of another big tree on fire. With a roar and a moan, a huge flaming branch snapped free and rolled towards them.

An unnaturally hot wind gusted down the slope as though also fleeing the hilltop. It was like being blasted by hell's hair dryer. Smoke rolled over them in waves, hissing like surf. She coughed as ash filled her lungs. The grit seemed to be settling in her stomach.

Anthea had often worried about life after death. Now she found herself worrying about life before death. Was she going to have any? The fire was racing down the slope towards them. Anthea started squeaking like a lost kitten.

Jacko grabbed her hand as they groped their way back towards the rushing river they'd just escaped from. Through eyes that were slitted against the smoke, she could see that the water had risen even higher.

'Jump in!'

Anthea looked at Jacko through the fug of fumes. A direct trip to downtown Kabul seemed like a better alternative than getting back into the roaring torrent. She tried to speak but the smoke made her throat seize up. Death, she realised, gasping, really is a breath-taking experience.

'On the count of three!' he yelled.

'NO!' she croaked.

'Get in!' he ordered.

Anthea glanced at the writhing river. There was no way she was getting back into the feverish floodwaters. If they were swept downstream, they'd be knocked out on the rocks. Or, worse, killed by a head-on collision. 'I'm not getting back into that river. I'd rather you shot a bullet through my brain,' she yelled back.

'Don't tempt me,' the big man barked. With that he seized her in a bear hug and leapt. The murky water thrashed around them. It was like getting into a washing machine. Jacko slid the belt free from his jeans and lassoed Anthea's waist. He then held her against an overhanging branch and tethered her to it. Water slapped against her legs and left them stinging.

'The fire should jump over us . . . ' All the bush behind them was now ablaze. The wall of heat was overwhelming. 'Are you okay?'

Okay? Anthea thought, astonished. *Okay?* He'd rolled the truck. She'd been nearly swept downstream and dashed to death on rocks, barbecued, and now drowned again . . . Yes,

Jacko had been quite heroic. But the whole hideous ordeal was his fault in the first damn place . . . If she *could* have spoken, it would have been to ask about how to say, in an Aboriginal language, 'Please make sure this man is mauled very slowly to death by dingoes.'

The river was now a bubbling soup of creatures, as kangaroos, wallabies, little bush rats, lizards and snakes all writhed and struggled in the rapids. Anthea clung to the branch. Waves smacked her in the face so repeatedly, she felt as though she was being interrogated by the Nazis. She jerked with alarm as she felt Jacko's strong body pressing her from behind, his arms stretching around her bra-less torso.

'What the hell do you think you are doing?' she croaked in her best school teacher voice.

'Protecting you, you idiot.'

The most dangerous thing Anthea had ever done before this was to park illegally in a loading zone. Overwhelmed by terror, she closed her eyes and prayed to a God she didn't really believe in, to please take some time off the Middle East and get her out of here.

Half way through her prayer, a primitive sense of dread electrified her nerves. Her skin prickled and crawled as though invisible creatures were creeping over it. She strained to see through the pall of smoke. As her eyes adjusted, the sensation that she was being watched intensified. And then she realised that two cold sinister eyes were staring directly into her face. She dug her nails into Jacko's arm. He yelped but then followed the direction of her gaze.

'Shit. A King Brown,' he said, quietly.

'K . . . King B . . . Brown?' Anthea stammered.

'One of the most poisonous and aggressive snakes in the world. Keep still.'

All Anthea could think about was how much nicer the snake would look as the belt of a cat-walk model. The King Brown had obviously been sheltering in the hollowed out section of the tree and had now slithered out on to the nearest branch. All three of them were marooned there, just looking at each other.

'What . . . what are you going to do?' Anthea squeaked.

'Gee, I don't know,' Jacko said sarcastically. 'Why don't I bend it into some fancy party-balloon shapes for you?'

He suddenly lunged for its tail. The snake hissed, fangs glistening. Moving with lightning speed (an expression Anthea only now fully understood, having nearly been toasted by Mother Nature earlier), he grabbed the snake by the tail, lassoed it in the air above his head and sent it flying. The snake arced through the air and into the churning stream. Anthea was astounded. This Jacko had more nerve than an unfilled tooth.

Upstream, flames were now leaping over the creek and igniting the dry trees on the opposite bank. Anthea choked and spluttered in horror. The fierce, scouring wind became ravenous, eating all in its path. Trees waved drunkenly, bent at crazy angles, their lush foliage now twisted and twined by the hot wind. As they caught fire, branches scratched like witches' fingers at the sky as if in pain.

This was it, Anthea thought. She was going to be roasted alive in the Aussie Outback. It was then that she started sobbing. The poor woman was weeping and wailing so hard, she didn't realise at first that her face was wet with raindrops and not tears. A great gunshot of thunder shuddered through the air. Cracking open one eye, she felt bewildered to find herself still alive.

She saw sombre clouds wrestling through the

smoky sky above them, bloated with rain. The burnt tree trunks, stripped bare of their leaves, stuck up like exclamation marks. And they had a lot to be alarmed about. Because right then the sky split open and it started to pour. It rained in torrents. The heavens seemed to be torn apart. This was obviously the storm that had caused the inland tsunami.

Anthea had never seen rain like it. It was end-of-the-world, Noah's Ark type rain. As the deluge dampened down the smoke, the bush hissed and smouldered around them. But the river was swelling even more. The branch they were clinging to was now half submerged. The earth around the trunk of the tree had been torn away, its exposed roots gnawed by the floodwaters.

'Okay. We need to make for the bank before this tree is swept away. Let go of the branch but keep hold of me,' Jacko ordered.

Anthea reacted as if he'd suggested taking out her teeth with pliers. 'No way!' she bleated. She wanted to trust him, but couldn't help feeling that getting back into the floodwaters would qualify her as the only living brain donor in human history.

Jacko untied the belt which tethered them to the branch and slid confidently into the current. He held on to the tree trunk and signalled for Anthea to also get back into the water. When she wouldn't let go, Jacko simply told her there was another snake making its way towards her. Needless to say, Anthea's entry into the water was a little less elegant than his had been. It was more like a walrus giving birth. After she'd spluttered and flailed on the surface and drunk a gallon or two of water, Jacko surfed to her side in a spritz of spray, then simply put her on his back and swam strongly for the bank.

The rain had turned the earth into the consistency of chocolate cake mix. It clung to her arms, legs, hair. This time it took a good ten minutes for her to clamber up the slippery slope beside the roaring torrent.

When she finally reached the top of the bank, a jolt of misery shot through her. Her sides ached. Her head hurt. Her ankles throbbed. Her teeth were chattering like Spanish castanets.

Jacko stood firmly before her, his muscular legs planted in a 'V'. 'I think we should take shelter under that ledge,' Jacko bellowed above the pounding rain.

'Really? I was actually just thinking about staggering off into the wilderness to die,' Anthea replied. But a crack of thunder changed her mind for her. She spun on her heel and bolted for the rock face as fast as her jarred ankle would take her – which was about half a step. She cried out in pain.

Jacko picked her up with ease and carried her to the red sandstone outcrop. He lowered her down gently on to the soft sand beneath the ledge. But she wasn't sheltered from the water pouring down the sides of the rock unless she crouched on a small patch of sand at the back. Anthea drew her knees up to her chest and tried to control her shivering.

'Are you having fun yet?' Jacko drawled, in an attempt to raise her flagging spirits. 'About as much fun as watching a couple of pensioners doing a pole dance, am I right?'

When she didn't respond, he charged off through the driving rain. A few moments later he returned, rolling a large boulder. He wedged it across the entrance to their small cave to protect her from the rain. Then he sat down beside her, legs akimbo.

'Jeez, Anthea. What a welcome to Australia,

eh? This kind of hospitality could hospitalise you!'

For the first time, she allowed herself to marvel openly at Jacko's practicality. She thought of Rupert then. He was not what you'd call practical. Her beloved didn't even know how to operate the TV remote. His only DIY procedure was the highly technical art of whacking the crap out of any electrical device that failed to start, to make it work again. He had once told her how relieved he was when wine bottles started to have twist tops, as even corkscrews were beyond him.

'The dying process begins the moment you come into the world – but it sure speeds up on a trip to Australia, doesn't it?' Jacko chuckled, still attempting to calm her frayed nerves.

Whether she was hysterical with shock or crazed with pain, she didn't know. But Anthea found herself snorting with laughter too. 'Packing for a visit to the Outback, I somehow overlooked the survival suit, inflatable raft and hot air balloon that are obviously essential in these parts.'

'Yep! Coming to the Outback leads to more early deaths than working as a stunt double, bullfighting and space travel all put together,' he chortled.

'Yes! Do come and stay Down Under. Give funeral directors more employment!' she giggled in reply.

They were both bent double with laughter now. Big heaving belly laughs rocked their frames. When they finally stopped to draw breath, Andrea realised that the rain was easing. The air was still leaden with humidity, though. Jacko kicked the boulder away with both feet to allow more oxygen into their cave. Anthea breathed in deeply. She could now see clouds scudding across the sky, like drying, grey laundry. Birds skimmed and wheeled over the swollen river. She started to speak. 'Mr Jackman, William . . . Bill . . .' she began, intending to thank him for rescuing her.

'Shhhh,' Jacko cut her off. Unexpectedly, he asked, 'Have you still got that lipstick on you?'

Anthea unzipped the pocket in her dress and dug down deep into the folds of soggy material. Unbelievably, the hard metallic tube was still there. Jacko snatched it from her. He rotated the shaft and a small mirror was revealed. He wriggled out of the cave and ran up the ridge of burnt land. At the top he angled the mirror at the sun. She watched, bemused, as he flashed out some secret semaphore.

'What are you doing?' she called out.

'Plane.'

Anthea peered at the heavens. And there it was – a small silver dart flying straight towards them.

'Dip your wing, you bastard. Dip!' Jacko pleaded.

For an unbearable stretch of time, the plane just soared on. The whole of the bush beneath seemed to hold its breath. Then, just when she thought she'd expire from anxiety, the plane miraculously tilted in their direction. Anthea's eyes widened and a sob of relief escaped her.

'You little beauty!' Jacko exclaimed. 'Eureka! You ripper! Fantastic! The pilot will wire our co-ordinates in to the cop shop. Big Bluey . . . he's our local policeman . . . will be here in no time. Bloody hell . . . more good luck! My backpack!' Jacko pointed to a battered tree at the river's edge. Wedged into the weed-strewn branches was a bedraggled Gore-Tex sack.

Jacko whooped with delight as he ran towards the tree. He shinned up into the branches and retrieved his bag. Back on the ground, he rummaged through its contents and extracted a small plastic bottle which he shook excitedly.

'Painkillers. I bet you're starting to feel those bruises taking hold . . . Here.' He flicked open the bottle with a thumbnail and popped two pills into his palm. 'Take these for the pain.'

Now that the immediate danger had subsided, Anthea realised she needed them. She could indeed feel an ache deep in her bones and a stiffness in her muscles. She examined her arms. Bruises were erupting all over her biceps. She imagined her legs and torso were in a similar condition.

Jacko gestured for her to lie back down on the dry sand of the cave. He sat beside her. Cupping her head, he helped her gulp down the pills.

'Are you okay?' He bent over her as though she was a lost puppy.

Anthea patted her body to make sure she had everything she'd started out with that morning. Then she nodded. 'Apart from my ankle. And my ribs.'

'Just rest now,' he ordered. Despite his cheeriness, the man's tired face looked as rumpled as an unmade bed.

Jacko gently examined her ankle. 'Sprained' was his verdict. He took off his shirt and bound it tightly about the swollen area. As the drugs kicked in, a pleasurable sensation spread over Anthea like melting butter. She became as docile as a child, allowing the half-naked miner to pull open her dress and tend to the gash on the side of her chest.

The sun and shade cast a mosaic of light and shadow on his face. She found herself drawn to this capable man, with his snake-handling skills and Harley-Davidson. Rupert would need trainer wheels on such a powerful motor bike. She remembered then once asking him to perform some maintenance task on her car. He'd reacted as though she'd given him instructions on how to fuel a nuclear reactor. Jacko was right. In a situation like this, Rupert would be as handy as a chocolate teapot.

Jacko, on the other hand, was the type of bloke who could take a cold remedy and still operate heavy machinery. With all her senses enhanced, she inhaled his warm spicy scent – a musky tang of petrol, sweat and cigarettes. Looking up at him, hazy with painkillers, it suddenly didn't seem strange to find him loveable. The nose she'd found coarse now appeared nobly Roman, the rough-hewn features chiselled. He wasn't gym toned, like Rupert, but corded by the kind of bulging muscles and sinews which only came from hard physical labour. And yet the strength of his body was at odds with his velvety fingertips.

'Your hands are so soft,' she marvelled, as he tended her wounds.

'I help out my mates with the shearing. It's the lanolin in the wool. You're lucky, Anthea. These cuts and scrapes are only superficial. Like me, eh?' He winked at her.

She realised now how warm his smile was. Jacko smiled with his whole face, especially his eyes.

Bandaging a cut on her upper arm, his hand grazed the pillowy softness of her breast. She was astonished to feel a fierce onrush of tenderness. The stillness of the Outback was like a theatre audience hushed in anticipation. But her mind was electric, filled with the present and the hot and resin-filled perfume of the bush. A dreamy sensuality took hold of her. The air felt solid, the weight of it pressing down on her. Her thoughts shimmered. She tilted her face up to him, like a sunflower turning towards the warmth. She found herself drifting in a trancelike state towards his mouth. She was all heat and need. In that instant, there was only one sensation – yes, now, yes.

'Yes, now, yes,' she heard a voice say, realising through her daze that the words were being uttered by her own mouth. Then she pressed his hand firmly against her naked breast.

Chapter Seven

Love Is Blind

The tense silence that followed was loud enough to make Anthea open her eyes. The look on Jacko's face registered more surprise than the congregation at Michael Jackson's wedding. He leapt back as though from the strike of a cobra. When he spoke he looked wary and disapproving.

'Your sister is a truly beautiful person,' was all he said.

'Yes. She is. Of course,' Anthea blurted, snapping out of her dreamy mood, her voice light and falsely cheery. The extent of his rejection hit her like a blow to the chest. A kookaburra bird cackled with contempt.

Anthea tried to smile but found she could not. She tried to apologise but her lips felt numb, as though she'd been to the dentist's. Jacko kept up his impression of a monk who has taken a vow of silence. He examined his hands with great attention to detail. A fraught hush fell over them both like red Outback dust.

Why on earth had she tried to kiss him? The desire had only lasted a moment before being swiftly replaced by the crippling shame of his rejection.

At the low rumbling sound of an approaching car, Anthea felt a knot of remorse in her stomach. She wanted to remind Jacko that he'd said thinking was over-rated and to go with her impulses . . . But his eyes were unreadable beneath the brim of his hat, his body language rigid and his disgust clear.

Jacko signalled to the police van. It was a dirt-covered utility truck with a cage on the back. It ground to a halt, with a squelch of mud. Jacko bounded over to greet the policeman. He wrenched open the truck door and shook the outstretched arm of the large uniformed man who was lumbering out of the driver's seat. The officer had long, scrawny legs, but a large belly shaped like a ball. He rolled when he walked, neck thrust forward like a bird of prey. Yet when he spoke to Jacko it was with affection.

'Jesus Christ, Jacko. What the bloody hell's

been going on? Where's that shit heap you call a car?'

'Probably in the Indian Ocean by now.' Jacko pointed to the swollen waters of the creek. 'Flash flood. Inland tsunami. Washed the old rust bucket right away.'

'What drama! The weather today's had more twists and turns than a bloody soap opera.'

'Just Mother Nature's mood swings . . . We even had a bolt from the blue. Can you believe it?'

'Jeez. No kidding? Hence the bush fire. We saw the smoke from town.'

'Luckily the storm put it out or we'd have been deep fried. Yep . . . It's been quite a day, one way and another.' Jacko cast a sidelong glance in Anthea's direction.

'Oh, hello there, Missy. I didn't see you there. And you are . . . ?' the officer asked her, screwing up his eyes with interest.

'Anthea. Jane's sister. From London,' she managed to say.

'Jane. Top bird! Can't believe she let you get into a truck with this maniac though,' the big man teased. 'He's an ugly bugger, isn't he? Looks as though his face caught fire and somebody tried to put it out with a shovel.'

'Not as ugly as the emu after it hit our windscreen. The truck rolled,' Jacko explained.

'Jeez. You were both lucky not to be killed. No broken bones?' Anthea shook her head. 'We'd better get you to the hospital for a check up. Just talk me through the accident first.'

While the officer took notes, Anthea tried to concentrate on his questions. She managed to reply but her mind was on Jacko. He was walking up and down the dirt road, scanning the horizon. When he saw another car crest the hill, he waved his arms in the air.

Jane leapt from the front seat while the wheels were still spinning. She threw herself at Jacko in joy and relief.

'Annie!' she yelled then, running to her sister's side. 'Are you okay?'

'Yes, yes, fine,' Anthea said in a quiet voice.

Jane laughed with relief, squeezing her close. 'Thank God! What a welcome to Australia! Are you sure you're okay?'

Jane was so concerned about her sister that the old tensions between them evaporated. Her warmth only served to increase Anthea's feelings of shame and guilt.

'I'm fine. Really. Fine.' Anthea's voice was

clipped and brittle, like a World War Two radio announcer.

Jane's face when she turned back to Jacko was naked in its love for him. She threw her arms around his neck again and hung and clung there.

'What a way to meet your brother-in-law. Don't judge him by this accident though. Jacko really is the most capable, clever, gorgeous man.'

'Yes,' Anthea said in her friendly sister tone, which sounded slightly false from disuse. 'I know.'

'I think I should get you to the hospital, young lady,' the policeman said to her. 'I've finished taking the statement. Unless there's anything else you want to tell me?'

Anthea's eyes were fixed on Jacko. Was he going to betray her?

'He's a rugged old bush cop, but he's kind,' Jane assured her sister, mistaking her anxiety for fear of a stranger. 'But we can take her to the doctor, Officer. In my car.'

'Okey-dokey,' the policeman agreed. 'You should get the doc to give you a once-over too, mate,' he advised Jacko. 'I'll get the main road cleared.'

Jacko nodded. He and the policeman slapped each other on the shoulder. As they said good-bye, Jane helped Anthea into the back seat of the car. She padded her head and back with cushions, strapped her into a seat belt, then slipped behind the wheel.

Anthea stretched her legs out along the back seat and pretended to sleep. Through half-closed eyes, she saw Jacko climb into the front passenger seat. She felt the car take his weight. She saw her sister's hand on Jacko's big meaty leg, her fingers covered by his strong hand. The engine started and Jane swung the car around. As they jolted and bounced over the rough bush track, Anthea listened to her sister, babbling happily, a brook of words, her laughter vibrant with affection and relief.

They drove on as night filled the car. Her sister's words washed over Anthea. She must have fallen into an uneasy sleep because when she opened her eyes it was to see Jane's smiling face directly above her. The neon hospital signs hurt Anthea's eyes, questioning her hard, accusing her of betraying her only sister.

'Help me, Jacko,' Jane asked. Together, they levered Anthea out of the back seat. Despite her remorse, as Jacko slid his strong hands under her armpits, she thrilled to his touch.

'Are you okay?' Jane asked again, disconcerted.

Anthea forced a smile. It was as sharp and sweet as icing, and as hard as the nails she was now digging into her palm. Jacko wouldn't catch her eye. Why had she tried to kiss him? She was engaged to the most perfect man on the planet.

Anthea, normally so clear-sighted, found that everything had blurred slightly for her. It was the shock of the crash obviously. But that didn't stop her from feeling that the mayor of this town had been right. Here Jane had become a beautiful swan and Anthea an ugly duckling. As soon as Jacko told Jane about her sister's behaviour, things would get very ugly indeed . . .

Chapter Eight

Love At Second Sight

In between being poked and probed by doctors, Anthea tried to ring Rupert. No answer. Where was he? She needed to speak to him so that she could take her romantic temperature, and soothe her nerves. Hearing his voice would remind her how much she loved him. The doctor gave her the all clear. If he'd used an emotional stethoscope he'd have seen her damaged heart. Despite the big, high room she was in, guilt pressed in on her like a low ceiling.

On the drive to Jacko's farm, silence wrapped her in its dark cloak. The tarmac was slick after the rain. Jacko put on the headlights. They reflected back harshly from the shining surface of the road.

Anthea was surprised by Jacko's quaint wooden farmhouse. It tilted slightly, as though tipsy. The corrugated iron of the roof creaked companionably in the wind. Once inside there were more surprises. The rooms were full of books and paintings and sculptures, with the music of a string quartet playing softly on the stereo. It was not at all what Anthea had expected. It also seemed to have been Jacko who had prepared the meal. As Jane unwrapped the kangaroo steaks, she raved about his gourmet cooking skills. There were lychee and lemon grass cocktails, with fish fillets to follow which he'd marinated in Thai spices. The only food Jane had made was the dessert – an old-fashioned bread and butter pudding, their mother's favourite, to remind them of home.

Anxious about leaving them alone, Anthea showered as quickly as she could and put on some of her sister's clothes. During dinner, Jacko and Anthea exchanged knowing glances. Anthea wondered desperately if Jacko had told Jane what she had done. But then surely her sister would not be so friendly now? Anthea arranged her face just so – not smiling, not sad, just attentive. Her usually sleek, blow-dried hair had frizzed up in the humidity. The big wavy mass allowed her to hide behind a curtain of hair.

Blaming jet lag, she finally gave up her vigil and retreated to her cool room above the courtyard and collapsed, sobbing into an old wrought-iron bed. Whenever she closed her eyes, the painful moment when she had tried to seduce her sister's fiancé was replayed endlessly on her mental screen. Her mind whirred and stopped, whirred and stopped, like a broken clock. Until, finally, she cried herself to sleep.

Anthea woke in the morning to the sound of her sister laughing. She looked into the courtyard to see Jane obviously telling a story and making over-the-top gestures as she did so. Jacko cackled delightedly, patting her hair and kissing her hand. Jane was one of those big, jokey girls with broad shoulders and chewed nails and cuticles. Yet the light around her seemed warmer somehow. Alluring.

Anthea joined them warily. Over brunch, Jacko's luminous eyes fleetingly held hers in a look of polite contempt. But Jane's eyes stayed summery with laughter, meaning he hadn't told her of their close encounter.

After they'd eaten, the sisters left Jacko cleaning up – another surprise, for Anthea, as Rupert never did the housework – and strolled by the creek. She had to lean on her younger sister because of her bandaged ankle. This reversal of roles unnerved her even more.

'So, you're happy for me?' Jane asked.

'I . . . I am.' They were shielded from the sun by the dappled shadow of some gum trees so Jane couldn't see the confusion in her sister's eyes.

'Jacko's house has a lot of character doesn't it? Like him.'

'Yes. Although I thought you'd be in a bigger place . . . '

Jane laughed. 'He doesn't know about my money. We're happy just the way we are.'

Anthea listened as if through a fog. 'I was wrong about Jacko,' she blurted suddenly. 'I was too quick to judge him,' she conceded. 'Maybe you were right about something else too . . . You don't need to grow up, Jane. I think I need to grow down.'

Jane looked at her sister with astonishment. 'You must be the first woman in the world who has been reincarnated *while still alive*,' she said.

Anthea and Jane smiled at each other, in a

cautious way. No longer enemies, they were un-sure how to speak to each other. And so they hugged, instead.

Chapter Nine

A Sight For Sore Eyes

For days Anthea lived on her nerves, waiting for her crime against her sister to be exposed. But Jane kept right on smiling. On the Sunday Jacko met up with his mates to take part in what they called the 'Undies 500'. The local miners and shearers, men Anthea had dismissed as selfish yobs, had dyed their hair red, blue, green and yellow, to raise money for a children's cancer charity. Locals had sponsored them to drive around all day in their underwear only. Anthea laughed, finally starting to appreciate the Aussie sense of humour, which was drier, she now realised, than the encroaching desert.

None of the racism she'd seen in the cab driver was apparent here. Jacko's mates included Aborigines, Asians, Pacific Islanders. These men, stripped down to their underpants, possessed the kind of strong, muscular frames rarely seen in London lawyers. Especially one young miner called Jimbo. Watching him flex and strut in nothing but a pair of skimpy undies (or what the locals called 'budgie smugglers'), Anthea understood why the tourist brochures boasted of the spectacular local views.

'I hope you're gonna come back for the wedding and give your sister away,' Jimbo encouraged her.

His choice of words seared Anthea. Jacko hadn't given *her* away. She had misjudged him so completely. Anthea could almost see her glib, unknowing, former self. Oh, how she despised that woman, with her foolish prejudices and pretensions. She knew nothing.

'Actually, it'd be kind of nice for us all if you could spend some more time out here,' Jimbo flirted with her. 'Your sister's already begun to think of Australia as home. Maybe you could too?' The handsome young bloke had a big grin, a firm handshake, a long stride and a wide smile. Not to mention his more private attributes. Put it this way, Jimbo filled out his underpants so well, she could detect the man's religion.

'I don't know. I've yet to be persuaded of the

charms of bush tucker,' Anthea found herself joking back. 'And it would be kind if certain people would stop teasing me about my accent.'

'What accent?' The handsome man grinned at her.

Driving back to the airport, the town didn't look as bad as it had done on first sight. There was a raw beauty to it that Anthea hadn't noticed before. The pub verandas were delicately fringed with iron 'lace'. The streets, originally built wide enough to allow old-fashioned carts drawn by bullocks to turn in them, were elegantly laid out. The red earth and blue sky reminded Anthea of paintings she'd seen by Salvador Dali. She half expected a face on stilts or a dripping clock to erupt from the landscape.

At the airline check-in desk, Jane embraced Anthea. 'If you can't make it back for the wedding, maybe you'll come for the christening . . .'

'You're pregnant?' Anthea was stunned. She felt a mix of emotions, joy and jealousy. She had always taken a secret pride in being more successful than her wayward little sister. But now it turned out that it was Jane who had made the real success of her life.

'We just found out. It's terrifying actually! But one thing I know for sure is that Jacko's going to make a great dad . . . I just wish Mum were around to hear the news,' Jane said sadly.

'Me too.' And then Anthea hugged her sister properly, for the second time in their adult lives.

Controlling her emotions, Jane thumped Jacko in the arm. 'He's an ugly devil. But, hey, you can't always judge by appearances.'

'At least you can no longer say that all the men who ever liked you for your sense of humour, ended up fancying me instead,' Anthea said, glancing sideways at Jacko.

'Anyway,' he replied good-naturedly, staring right back at Anthea as if seeing straight through her, 'ugliness is purely in the eye of the beholder. You can get it out with Optrex drops.'

His remark stung her. Anthea felt furious with herself. Stranded out there in the bush, she had lost her balance, that was all. She'd been teetering like a tight-rope walker . . . and had momentarily fallen from grace.

By the time she had settled into her seat on board the aircraft, she felt her old self returning. It wasn't fair of Jacko to judge her. She'd been terrified, jet lagged and drugged up on painkillers. Kissing him had been a mistake, that was all. Rough diamonds like him were all very well, she thought to herself, as she sipped champagne in the first-class cabin, but she liked her men with a little polish. As the plane taxied down the runway, the whole experience began to feel like a mirage to her.

They took off and turned towards Perth. The intensity of the last few days faded away as fast as the mining town below. Eventually her sister and Jacko were both just a blip on the horizon so far as Anthea was concerned. All she could think about now was boarding the flight to London and returning to the safety of her side of the world, her home, her beloved.

Chapter Ten

Love May Be Blind, But Marriage Is A Real Eye Opener

In her absence London seemed to have changed from sparkling European gem to grubby fake jewel. The city, smeared by car fumes, looked grey and grimy. Pedestrians seemed to hurry everywhere like caged mice. And the sky appeared to be falling in. After the big blue expanse of the Australian Outback, the London sky felt alarmingly low.

'Darling!' Rupert glanced up from his spotless glass desk – which looked, now Anthea thought about it, like a case in a museum. She was about to recount the details of her accident when he interrupted. 'Notice anything?' He leant back in his posture-correct chair. 'No glasses!' he said, before she could answer. 'I had my eyes lasered. It's almost Biblical . . . "I can see! I can see"!' he joked.

'But I liked your Clark Kent look,' Anthea said, feeling baffled. 'Why didn't you talk it over with me first?'

'I wanted it to be a little surprise. I had to take a week off to recover.'

'But you said the reason you couldn't come with me was because you were busy selling your shares so that we could buy a house.'

Rupert got up from his desk, crossed the room and slipped one arm around her waist. 'Ah, well, yes, but the prices fell. It wasn't the right time to sell. We'll just wait another six months or so . . . maybe a year . . .'

Anthea's heart sank down into her shoes. 'So, while I was out in the bush, trying to save my sister, nearly being killed by feral emus and floods and bush fires, you were merely getting your eyes lasered?'

'It was supposed to be a surprise. I booked in for surgery months ago. I didn't want to cancel . . . What do you think?'

What Anthea thought was that their carefully designed, earth-toned apartment lacked character. It was seared by light yet freezing cold. Winter and summer, Rupert liked the thermostat set to Arctic level. She missed the Outback heat, the air thick with abundant birds and insects. The browny-green carpet Rupert had imported from Italy now looked to her like creeping mould. His discarded tie lay in a tired snarl of silk on the chair.

'And to tell the truth, I wasn't entirely convinced you needed to go on your mission, Annie. Jane's miner may be rough and ready, but to be frank, with her looks, who else was she going to attract? I thought the only thing she'd ever have between her legs would be that ridiculous cello.' He laughed at his own joke.

'Jane is a highly intelligent, artistic woman,' Anthea objected. 'Are looks all that count with you men? When they say beauty comes from within, Rupert, they do *not* mean from within a jar marked Estée Lauder.'

'I hate to think what their children will look like. I just hope they have a life guard by their gene pool,' he continued.

Anthea bristled, and not just because of the insult to her sister. She'd always presumed she and Rupert would be the first to have a child.

Her sister's news had left her reeling. And now Repert wanted to put off having a family yet again.

Rupert misread her upset mood. 'I'm only joking, Annie. Did you leave your sense of humour at Customs? I think you must just be a little tired after your trip out to that hellhole.' He massaged her shoulders. 'How bad was it?'

'Actually, it has its own beauty – the bush.'

Rupert slid the silk top she was wearing off her shoulders and nibbled her neck. 'Not as beautiful as you.'

'I've been trying to call you for days but there was no answer. So many things happened . . .'

'Oh, yes. So sorry, darling. There was no signal at the clinic in the country. And I was quite doped up on painkillers.'

'I needed to talk to you . . . I . . .'

'Why not let our bodies do the talking? Let's make love, right here, looking out over the river.'

The touch of his fingers on her skin felt so soothing. She sighed with relief and pleasure as he caressed her. Her irritability melted away. She kissed him back with passion. Perhaps she was just a little jet lagged after her trip. Rupert knelt to peel down her jeans, but his head jerked back like a snake surprised by a mirror. 'Is that . . . is that . . . cellulite? Good God, I never noticed that before.'

Anthea's fiancé began to examine her thighs with such intensity that she felt like a new strain of bacteria beneath a microscope. 'How long have you had cellulite?' he asked playfully, but his gaze was reproachful. 'Come to think of it, I've never really seen you naked before. My eyesight was so bad and I always took my glasses off when we made love. Well, well, well . . . Who's been letting herself go?' He addressed her as though she were a stray cat which had wandered into the garden.

Anthea felt a shift in her feelings for her fiancé. It was as though she'd woken up to find that all the furniture in the flat had been rearranged without her knowledge.

Before she had time to adjust, Rupert pulled her down on to the carpet by the mirror in his study. 'My word, Annie, what were they feeding you out there?' He gave her three pats on her rump, the sort you would give an old dog. 'Somebody needs to tone up! Now that I've had laser surgery, there's no pulling the wool over my eyes any more.'

The man she'd thought she adored began to go a little blurry for her, like a smudged watercolour or a photo taken slightly out of focus.

After they'd made love, when she glanced across at him to gauge his reaction to the slight bruises and scratches on her upper arms, Rupert was looking at her as though she were a carb-laden, full-fat burger his doctor had told him to avoid, instead of the organic beet salad he'd actually ordered.

'Perhaps you need a better jogging bra, babe. Haven't you ever noticed those stretch marks on your breasts? I've never seen them before. Did you ever notice them?' His tone was one of baffled disappointment.

Thoughts crowded her mind like traffic. 'One day I will have nipples down to my knees, you know. What will you think then?'

'There's always cosmetic surgery. Beauty is, after all, one of the most natural and lovely things money can buy,' he joked. But there was no warmth in his voice.

'I see. So, are our wedding vows going to say "For better or for worse – but not if your secretary is prettier and predatory"?'

'Of course not, darling,' he said, but his smile

did not quite reach his eyes. He pulled her to him again and tried to distract her with kisses.

She attempted a caress in return, but her lover seemed to be disappearing before her eyes, melting slowly like a snowman until all that was left of him was a pool of ice. He'd noticed her flaws but not the many fading scratches and bruises on her body from her near-death experience. As he entered her again, this time from behind, she glanced up over her shoulder and caught Rupert looking appreciatively into the mirror – at himself.

It was then that Anthea's mild anxiety changed entirely into revulsion. She couldn't hide a swift shudder of disgust. 'Epiphany' – an enormous breath of understanding – was the word she would use later to Jane. Her fiancé obviously kept fit by doing step aerobics off his own ego. Her sister was right. The man had love bites on his mirror. Rupert might have been the one to have eye surgery, but it was Anthea's vision which was suddenly, miraculously, clear. They'd been so keen to get an apartment that looked out over the Thames, they had forgotten to take a good long look at each other.

In the evening sun the river became a shining mirror – and Anthea didn't like what she saw in it. Namely that the scratches on her were not the only superficial things about her. She'd been emotionally short-sighted. *She* was the one who needed her eyesight adjusted. She couldn't believe she'd ever seen anything in Rupert. Or how blinkered she'd been to his faults. The rushing tidal waves of the Thames smacked against the embankment wall, as though scolding her for her stupidity.

Rupert stopped stroking her thigh and flicked at a patch of dry skin. 'Maybe you need a body scrub, babe? Or a day at the spa or something? Your skin is so dry, it's audible!'

Her angry expression evaporated into a look of distant, almost sweet, unconcern. 'Really? My clever sister has found the perfect cure for that. Lanolin.' Anthea thought quickly. If she gave in her notice at work, kicked out Rupert and sold the flat, that would give her three weeks in which to get back to Australia for Jane's wedding. And time to convince Jacko that she was sorry for what she'd done, and that there was more to her than met the eye. How astounded Jane would be to see Anthea do something spontaneous for once! Jimbo had promised to take her caving, horse riding, panning for gold . . .

She slapped away Rupert's hand and crossed the room to switch off the air conditioning and throw open a window. 'Oh, a little hint to help you find your next girlfriend, Rupert,' she said over her shoulder. 'Ugliness is purely in the eye of the beholder. You can get it out with Optrex.'

Books in the Quick Reads series

 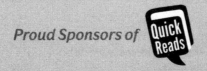

Start a new chapter

Quick Reads are brilliant short new books by bestselling
authors and celebrities. We hope you enjoyed this one!

Find out more at **www.quickreads.org.uk**

🐦 @Quick_Reads   📘 Quick-Reads

We would like to thank all our funders:

We would also like to thank all our partners in the Quick Reads project
for their help and support: NIACE, unionlearn, National Book Tokens,
The Reading Agency, National Literacy Trust, Welsh Books Council,
The Big Plus Scotland, DELNI, NALA

At Quick Reads, World Book Day and World Book Night
we want to encourage everyone in the UK and Ireland
to read more and discover the joy of books.

World Book Day is on 7 March 2013
Find out more at **www.worldbookday.com**

World Book Night is on 23 April 2013
Find out more at **www.worldbooknight.org**

Why not start a Quick Reads reading group?

If you have enjoyed this book, why not share your next Quick Read with friends, colleagues, or neighbours.

A reading group is a great way to get the most out of a book and is easy to arrange. All you need is a group of people, a place to meet and a date and time that works for everyone.

Use the first meeting to decide which book to read first and how the group will operate. Conversation doesn't have to stick rigidly to the book. Here are some suggested themes for discussions:

- How important was the plot?

- What messages are in the book?

- Discuss the characters – were they believable and could you relate to them?

- How important was the setting to the story?

- Are the themes timeless?

- Personal reactions – what did you like or not like about the book?

There is a free toolkit with lots of ideas to help you run a Quick Reads reading group at **www.quickreads.org.uk**

Share your experiences of your group on Twitter 🐦 @Quick_Reads

For more ideas, offers and groups to join visit Reading Groups for Everyone at **www.readingagency.org.uk/readinggroups**

Enjoy this book?

Find out about all the others at **www.quickreads.org.uk**

For Quick Reads audio clips as well as videos and ideas to help you enjoy reading visit **www.bbc.co.uk/skillswise**

Join the Reading Agency's Six Book Challenge at **www.readingagency.org.uk/sixbookchallenge**

THE READING AGENCY

Find more books for new readers at **www.newisland.ie** **www.barringtonstoke.co.uk**

Barrington Stoke
cracking reading

Free courses to develop your skills are available in your local area. To find out more phone 0800 100 900.

For more information on developing your skills in Scotland visit **www.thebigplus.com**

Want to read more? Join your local library. You can borrow books for free and take part in inspiring reading activities.